GW01454556

# Synchronicity

# Also by Keira Andrews

## Contemporary

*Honeymoon for One*
*Beyond the Sea*
*Ends of the Earth*
*Arctic Fire*
*The Chimera Affair*

## Holiday
*Only One Bed*
*Merry Cherry Christmas*
*The Christmas Deal*
*Santa Daddy*
*In Case of Emergency*
*Eight Nights in December*
*If Only in My Dreams*
*Where the Lovelight Gleams*
*Gay Romance Holiday Collection*

## Sports
*Kiss and Cry*
*Reading the Signs*
*Cold War*
*The Next Competitor*
*Love Match*
*Synchronicity* (free read!)

## Gay Amish Romance Series
*A Forbidden Rumspringa*
*A Clean Break*
*A Way Home*
*A Very English Christmas*

**Valor Duology**
*Valor on the Move*
*Test of Valor*
*Complete Valor Duology*

**Lifeguards of Barking Beach**
*Flash Rip*
*Swept Away* (free read!)

# Historical

*Kidnapped by the Pirate*
*Semper Fi*
*The Station*
*Voyageurs* (free read!)

# Paranormal

**Kick at the Darkness**
*Kick at the Darkness*
*Fight the Tide*

*Taste of Midnight* (free read!)

# Fantasy

**Barbarian Duet**
*Wed to the Barbarian*
*The Barbarian's Vow*

# SYNCHRONICITY

BY KEIRA ANDREWS

*Synchronicity*

© **2013 Keira Andrews**
Print Edition

All rights reserved. This book or any portion thereof may not be reproduced or used in any manner whatsoever without the express written permission of the author or publisher except for the use of brief quotations in a book review.

**ISBN:** 978-1-988260-72-3

**Cover by** Dar Albert
**Formatting by** BB eBooks

This is a work of fiction. Names, characters, businesses, places, events and incidents are either the products of the author's imagination or used in a fictitious manner. No persons, living or dead, were harmed by the writing of this book. Any resemblance to any actual persons, living or dead, or actual events is purely coincidental.

Diving icon made by Freepik from www.flaticon.com is licensed under CC BY 3.0

# DIVE 1

"READY?"

"Yeah."

"Up."

Perched backwards on the edge of the platform, heart thumping, Tyler raised his arms over his head. With the adrenaline flowing, he didn't even feel the ache in his back that had kept him awake half the night. He tried not to think about the fact that the whole world was watching, and closed his eyes.

*Just another day at the pool.*

"Ready?" Aiden asked again.

Their heels hung over the side, ten meters above the glistening surface of the pool as they took identical starting positions. The fear burned in Tyler's chest and what-ifs ricocheted through his mind before he could silence them. *I've done this a thousand times. It won't happen again. It was a fluke.*

"Yeah."

"One, two, three—go."

1

Tyler bent his knees and exploded up off the platform, straightening his legs and folding his body forward at the waist in the pike position. As he and Aiden fell in unison, he put his arms above his head and straightened out in plenty of time to slice into the water with as little splash as possible, his body vertical, bruised toes pointed painfully.

They plunged into the pool, and Tyler flipped upright and swam to the edge next to Aiden. He hoisted himself out and hurried over to the showers on the wall behind the diving platform, ignoring the twinges from his toes as adrenaline flooded him. *I did it.*

His first Olympic dive was in the books.

It had felt like a good one—and the crowd certainly thought so, if their enthusiastic applause was any gauge. He chanced a smile at Aiden, who nodded, a smile briefly lifting his full lips. Aiden reached out his hand and they slapped their palms together lightly.

Eyes closed, Tyler stepped under the warm water. As he turned, his shoulder brushed against Aiden's, sending a delicious shiver up his spine. God, how he wanted to wrap his arms around him and feel his powerful body from head to toe, press their lips together and…

*What else is new?*

With a rueful chuckle under his breath, Tyler opened his eyes and stepped out from under the shower. *This is the Olympic Games. Focus.*

Five dives to go.

Five days earlier

"PENNY FOR YOUR thoughts. Or a nickel, I guess, since they don't make pennies anymore."

Aiden glanced away from the bus window, his pensive expression disappearing under the mask of a smile. "Just thinking. Aren't you sitting back there with the swimmers?"

"Nah. Too rowdy for me." Tyler plopped down next to Aiden, jostling against him slightly as the bus pulled out. He knew Aiden probably wanted to be alone like usual, but Tyler wanted to share this experience. Not that Aiden ever said he wanted to be alone, but the only time Tyler saw him outside the pool was when they travelled to competitions. "But I can go back if you want."

"No, of course not. Don't mind me. Can't shut my brain off sometimes."

"But this is still supposed to be fun, right? Can't we worry about the competition after the opening ceremony?"

"Yeah, of course." Aiden shrugged. "Besides, there's nothing to worry about. We'll do our best and whatever happens, happens."

Tyler pushed away a flicker of irritation. He knew they shouldn't get their hopes up, but he still wished Aiden had more confidence in their partnership. "Yeah, but we at least have a *shot* at the podium. We've been diving really well. Don't you think?"

Aiden nodded. "Yeah. Like I said, we'll do our best." He gazed out at the jubilant crowds.

"I guess this is old hat for you now."

"No way." Aiden's smile seemed real this time. "This may be my second Olympics, but I don't think it'll ever get old."

It was on the tip of Tyler's tongue to ask why Aiden had seemed so sad a moment ago—as he often did when he thought Tyler wasn't looking. Of course, little did Aiden know that Tyler watched him every chance he got. He knew it was a hopeless crush, but he couldn't help himself. "Aiden—"

"Yoooooo!" Mike Grantwell had ventured up from the swimmers' party at the back of the bus. No one would dare break training and drink before their competitions, but the energy of the Games provided a natural high.

"Hey, Mike." Tyler raised his hand to return Mike's high five. "I thought you guys were supposed to be skipping the ceremony. Aren't you competing tomorrow?"

"The backstrokers are, but the rest of us have a few days. Thank God. No way I'm missing this." He motioned to the packed streets. "Look at all the hot chicks." He winked. "You two are gonna clean up in the Village. I swear, you guys are brothers from another mother. You sure you're not related?"

"We're sure," Tyler answered. They'd heard it a million times since their coaches paired them up six months earlier.

"I can barely tell you apart."

"That's because you're an idiot, Mike." Nathalie Bourbeau piped up from the seat in front, but there was no venom in the insult. "So, how many swimmers does it take to screw in a light bulb?"

Mike guffawed. "How many?"

Nathalie shrugged. "We don't know yet. They keep getting electrocuted."

Beside Nathalie, her partner Audrey giggled, and they all laughed. Mike waved his hand. "Yeah, yeah. You divers are just as wet as we are."

"The difference is we're smart enough to towel off before changing light bulbs," Nathalie replied with a wink before she and Audrey returned to chattering in French.

As Mike was called back to re-join the swimmers, the bus neared the stadium, winding its way through downtown Toronto. The streets teemed with people, many waving Canadian flags and wearing red. With each block closer, Tyler's pulse increased. He was about to walk into the opening ceremony of the freaking *Olympics* as part of the home team. He took a deep breath. "I don't know why I'm so nervous."

"Because a billion people around the world are going to be watching?" Aiden ran a hand through his dirty-blond hair and put on his red cap. "We're all nervous. But this is the fun part." He nodded toward the looming dome, which was open to the balmy night. "Look, we're here."

Tyler put on his own cap over his light blond hair and they filed off the bus to join their other teammates in the bowels of the stadium, where the Parade of Nations would begin. As host nation, Canada went last, and some of the other countries had already taken their lap. The athletes gathered as more buses arrived, filling up the area. The din of the crowd's cheers above them hummed in the air.

In their matching uniforms, Tyler mused that he and Aiden really could be brothers. At five nine they were both tall for divers, which made them a natural fit as synchro partners. Aiden's shoulders were a bit broader, but they had similar body types—muscular, yet lean. Their only major physical difference was the blue of Tyler's eyes, while Aiden's were a dark brown. They both even had dimples in their cheeks when they smiled. As Nathalie put it once, they were "*très* Abercrombie."

But Aiden's *real* smiles were few and far between, and once again Tyler found himself chewing over what was bothering him. Of course their partnership had been the last thing either had expected, and

Tyler knew he couldn't fill Greg Lewis's shoes. He'd tried his best, but Aiden must be wishing it was Greg with him at this Olympics.

Little Nathalie nudged Tyler with her elbow, grinning. "Can you believe it? We're really here! We did it!"

Putting thoughts of Aiden aside momentarily, Tyler slung his arm over Nathalie's shoulders and gave her a squeeze. They'd trained together in Montreal for three years before Tyler had gotten the call to go to Calgary. At twenty, they were the youngest members of the team, and Tyler was very glad to have Nathalie with him.

She frowned and lowered her voice as she tucked a dark curl behind her ear. "What is it?"

Before he could answer, she raised her eyebrows. "Wait—three guesses, and the first two don't count."

"*Nat.*"

Smiling, she shook her head and leaned in to whisper. "Don't worry. Your secret's safe with me."

Tyler knew that was true, and pressed a kiss to her cheek as officials called for attention and the athletes clustered together in groups, with the veterans and flag bearer taking the lead. When Canada was announced, the roaring in the stadium reached a fevered pitch, rolling over them like a wave. In this moment, standing next to Aiden, Tyler had never felt more proud. It took everything in him not to reach for Aiden's hand.

As the athletes ahead of them began walking up the concrete ramp, Tyler took a deep breath and touched Aiden's arm lightly. They all wore long-sleeved red jackets over khaki pants, but Tyler swore he felt a bolt of electricity where they touched. "Thank you."

Aiden blinked. "For what?"

*For being the most incredibly smart and kind and sexy man I've ever met, even if you'll never like me in the same way.* "I don't know. For everything. I'm so glad I'm here with you."

An emotion Tyler couldn't identify flickered across Aiden's face. "Me, too."

Then they were marching, and even though deep down Tyler felt Aiden was only being nice, he wanted to believe it. The crowd screamed as they entered the stadium, cheers and love echoing in the warm night air. As he grinned and waved, Tyler let himself be swept away with Aiden at his side.

# DIVE 2

T HE AUDIENCE CHEERED for the Chinese team's high marks, but Tyler blocked it out, breathing in and out steadily. He and Aiden stood with heads high and shoulders back atop the platform, waiting to take their positions. His body ached, but he ignored that too. This was the Olympics and he just had to focus. Mind over matter.

When it was time, Aiden gave the command to walk and they turned to hang their heels over the edge of the platform.

"Ready?"

"Yeah."

Aiden gave the next directive in the sequence. "Up."

Tyler raised his arms to shoulder height.

"Ready?"

He concentrated on breathing. "Yeah."

"One, two, three—go."

They jumped into the air for the backwards dive,

pulling their legs up and reaching for their toes before unfolding and entering the water. Their coaches whistled and the audience hooted and hollered. This time they both headed for the nearby hot tub, and Tyler tried to pretend he wasn't anxiously waiting for the scores.

When the 9.0s flashed up across the board for execution and synchronicity, Tyler exhaled. As the last team, the Mexicans, performed their second dive, Tyler watched the results board from the corner of his eye. For the moment they were in third place behind the favored Chinese and Americans, but the up-and-coming Mexicans could overtake them.

Another diver climbed into the hot tub, and Tyler scooted over. His leg hit Aiden's beneath the water, and their thighs brushed together. Aiden didn't move away, and Tyler's stomach flip-flopped. Just then, the crowd screamed its approval, and he glanced back up.

*3. OXFORD Aiden / BOURNE Tyler*

Still in third place. Four dives to go.

*Four days earlier*

"OXFORD AND BOURNE." The official at the front of the small meeting room called their names.

Tyler glanced at Aiden sitting beside him. "You sure you want me to draw?"

"Go for it." Aiden gave him a fist bump.

With a deep breath, Tyler walked to the front of the room. He pulled up the sleeve of his uniform shirt, although it wasn't necessary considering there were only a few slips of paper left in the bowl. He resisted the urge to fondle every slip, searching for the perfect one, and pulled out the first one he touched. He handed it to the official.

"Seven," the woman said.

There was a smattering of polite applause, and Tyler returned to his seat. "I guess it's okay?"

Aiden smiled. "It's fine. There are only eight teams anyway. We're not first and we're not last. It's a good spot."

When the draw was finished, it was time to meet with the press. Everyone on the Canadian team had attended media training, but Tyler was hoping to leave most of the talking to Aiden as they took their spots and the first reporter approached.

The woman smiled with glossy lips. "Aiden, how nice to see you again. Tyler, it's a pleasure to meet you."

Aiden smiled mechanically. "Hi, Theresa. We're thrilled to be here."

Theresa went right for the jugular. "Aiden, you and Greg Lewis just missed the podium four years ago and were expected to be gold medal contenders together here in Toronto. Will you be testifying at Greg's hearing in October?"

Tyler glanced at Aiden nervously. The last thing they needed was for the media to dredge up the unpleasant details of Greg's steroid use and upset Aiden. But Aiden appeared as stoic as ever, his expression placid.

"If I'm called. But right now I'm concentrating on these Games and doing my best to help Team Canada."

"As Greg's partner for so many years, do you feel there's still a cloud of suspicion hanging over you although you've never tested positive for banned substances? And even now that you're diving with Tyler?"

Tyler blurted out, "Aiden's passed every test in the book with flying colors. No one who's checked the facts suspects him of any wrongdoing. If you think—"

One of the team officials stepped in and, with a tight smile on her face, put her hand on Tyler's shoulder. She leaned in and spoke quietly with Theresa, who nodded and turned her gleaming smile on Tyler. "At only twenty years old, how does it feel to be at your first Olympics?"

With a deep breath, Tyler forced himself to smile and let his anger go. "It feels amazing. I'm so excited to be here in Toronto representing my country, especially since I grew up only an hour away."

"Do you feel added pressure having these Games at home?"

*Abso-fucking-lutely.* "Not at all. We've gotten so much love and support from our friends and family and the whole country. The only pressure comes from ourselves."

"But of course you've had to step up and fill some big shoes. You've only been competing at the senior level for a year. It must be nerve-wracking!"

Tyler resolutely kept smiling. "I'm going to do my best." He knew what a disappointment it would be to Aiden and the team if they didn't medal because of Tyler.

"Having a veteran partner must help. Aiden, at twenty-seven, how does it feel to be the old man of the team?"

Aiden chuckled. "It feels great. I know I speak for Tyler and everyone when I say we've all worked hard and we can't wait to compete."

Theresa pointed to the chain around Aiden's neck. "Can I ask about your necklace? You wear it everywhere but in the pool."

Aiden dutifully tugged the small, silver medallion out from beneath his shirt. "It's a St. Sebastian medal my parents gave me years ago. He's the patron saint of archers, athletes and soldiers. As athletes we certainly feel a lot like soldiers sometimes."

Theresa nodded to her photographer, who snapped a photo. Then her expression grew serious.

"Tyler, after Andrea May's terrible accident at the U.S. Olympic trials, are you nervous about diving off that platform? Ten meters is a long way up, and as we saw in Nashville, the slightest miscalculation can be catastrophic."

Images of the American diver plummeting to the water and the blood staining the pool deck afterwards as the paramedics worked on her flickered through Tyler's mind. He'd tried to resist watching the clip of the accident online, but a sick curiosity had gotten the better of him.

He concentrated on his rote answer. "We all know the risks. Accidents happen in every aspect of life, including diving, unfortunately. We're here to do our jobs, and we have to put that out of our minds. But we wish Andrea all the best in her recovery. She's a tough competitor and I'm sure she'll be back for the next Games."

As Aiden chimed in to echo Tyler's statements, Tyler tried to banish the images of Andrea's fall. He'd seen the replay, and her approach had looked totally fine. But she'd gone up too close to the platform and cracked the top of her head against the side as she rotated down. For a week he'd second guessed every move he made until realizing that would be the thing that got him hurt.

"Aiden, you're also competing in singles in the platform competition. At the trials, you were first and Tyler, you were fourth. Is there any rivalry between you?"

"Not at all," Tyler answered honestly. "I'll be cheering for Aiden harder than anyone."

Theresa leaned in conspiratorially. "All right, I just have to ask one more question. It's something our readers have all wondered about. Do those teeny tiny Speedos ever come off during a dive?"

They laughed good-naturedly, and Tyler grinned. "Believe it or not, those suits are stuck to us like glue."

"Don't you feel practically naked up there? Not that you don't have amazing bodies to show off."

Aiden jumped in. "Thanks, Theresa. We're used to it, so we don't really give it any thought."

"One more question: Do you have any waxing tips? Because it looks like you boys take it *all* off."

They smiled stiffly because they had to, and Tyler couldn't help but blush. Of course they did wax their entire bodies to cut down on resistance entering the water, but waxing his junk wasn't something he wanted to talk about with the world.

Theresa's time was up, and a parade of other journalists came by to ask similar questions. When it was over, Tyler sighed in relief and checked the time. "Are you coming to lunch with my parents?"

"Nah, I don't want to intrude. Go catch up and have some quality time. I'll see you at practice this afternoon."

Tyler couldn't help the pang of disappointment.

It was true that he hadn't seen his parents since March, but it felt like Aiden was holding Tyler at arm's length, as usual. "When are your parents flying in?"

"Day before the competition." Aiden pulled his phone from his pocket and tapped the screen. "Hey, is whatshisname coming?"

Tyler frowned. "Who?"

Aiden didn't look up from his phone. "You know. Tony?"

Tyler laughed. "*Tony*? No. I haven't seen him in ages."

"Oh. I thought you guys were dating." Aiden's brows drew together.

"Yeah, for five minutes. He was nice and all, but who has time for that?"

Aiden laughed tightly. "Tell me about it. Okay, see ya later." With a wave, he was gone.

As Tyler made his way to the buses to catch a lift downtown, he pondered Aiden's question. He was amazed Aiden even remembered Tony's name. Tyler had met him during a rare trip to the bar for another diver's birthday party. They'd gotten off furtively together in the bathroom, but Tyler hadn't planned on seeing him again. It was sweet when Tony then surprised him by showing up at the pool to take him to dinner, but Tyler had to let him down gently that evening.

Not only did he not have the time with training

and his correspondence courses from McGill in Montreal, but the only man Tyler really wanted was Aiden. When he'd groped Tony in the bathroom stall, he'd imagined it was Aiden.

And of course Aiden and his firm ass starred in all of Tyler's jerk-off fantasies. It seemed cruel that Tyler spent the majority of his days half-naked and wet with Aiden, yet their relationship was strictly platonic.

Tyler had fooled around with his fair share of guys, but never really had a boyfriend. He'd had a girlfriend in grade eight, but even then he'd known he was gay, and his parents knew it too. He laughed to himself. It hadn't taken his girlfriend long to figure it out either, with the way Tyler had drooled over her Britpop pinups.

For his part, Aiden didn't seem to be dating, either. Tyler was pretty sure Aiden was gay too, but Aiden kept his private life very private. Even in the insular diving world, there was hardly any gossip about him—in terms of dating, at least. Of course, when the situation with Greg had exploded, that was all anyone could talk about.

As he took his seat on the athletes' bus, Tyler shook his head and told himself to stop obsessing over Aiden for a change. He was going to have lunch with his parents and not think about Aiden at all.

He lasted about ten seconds, but called it a victory.

# DIVE 3

★★ 🤿 ★★

WITH EACH STEP closer to the top of the platform, Tyler's palms tingled and he focused on breathing steadily. Like all the teams, their first two dives had been relatively easy, with a 2.0 degree of difficulty. The third round was where the competition really began, with dives upwards of 3.0 being the norm.

Their coaches' voices echoed in his mind, reminding him that this was just another day at the pool, and to do it like they did in training. Panic flickered through Tyler as they reached the top. He thought of the thousands of successful dives he'd done over the years without hitting the platform.

Suddenly every dive that ever went wrong in his entire life played out in his mind like a slideshow, from belly flopping into his grandparents' pool to hitting his forehead on the springboard at the junior nationals when he was twelve.

*Enough!*

Again, they made their approach and took their positions on the edge of the platform, this time for an inward three-and-a-half somersault. Tyler was so glad he wasn't alone. Aiden's presence beside him was a steady comfort, and he homed in on Aiden and on breathing in time with him. They readied themselves and got into position.

"One, two, three—go."

Tyler propelled himself up, getting good elevation before quickly assuming the tuck position, hugging his knees to his chest to complete the revolutions before opening up for a rip entry. It felt clean, and as always he hoped there hadn't been much splash. He bumped fists with Aiden as they hurried to the hot tub. Tyler couldn't help but wince as he walked despite the rush of adrenaline.

Aiden murmured as they sat down in the warm water. "Toes?"

"Just aching a bit. Nothing to worry about."

"Back?"

"Same."

"You can do it." Aiden squeezed Tyler's knee briefly.

God, Tyler wanted to lean into Aiden's warmth, feel the slick slide of his skin and the strength of his arms and—*focus*. Nodding, he smiled, mindful of all the eyes and cameras on them. He could do it. He *would* do it.

Three dives left.

*Three days earlier*

WITH A SIGH, Tyler flipped over onto his other side and cursed himself for not bringing earplugs. Although it was after midnight, the Olympic Village pulsed with energy. Above the hum of the air conditioning, he heard snatches of laughter and the low thump of music.

Turned out that when you put thousands of young, fit people together, it was like an episode of *The Bachelor* on crack. People were hooking up left, right and center. As the Games went on and athletes completed their events, the Village was becoming a non-stop party zone. Tyler had slept well the other nights, but now, for some reason, the harder he tried, the more awake he felt.

After flipping onto his back and straightening the sheets, Tyler let his hand drift below the waist of his boxers without thinking. Usually when he couldn't sleep, he'd jerk off to lull himself into slumber. He froze and glanced over at Aiden's bed. Aiden was sprawled on his stomach, fast asleep with lips parted. He looked peaceful—the usual furrow between his brows smooth, the sadness gone.

The ever-present desire for Aiden flooded Tyler's veins, and before he could think better of it he had licked his palm and was stroking himself. He knew he should at least have a modicum of decency and go to the bathroom to get off, but as he touched himself, Tyler couldn't tear his eyes away from Aiden.

The sheet was slung low on Aiden's hips, and his boxers had slid down to expose a sliver of the pale curve of his ass. They'd closed the blinds on the window, but enough light from the bright lamps illuminating the walking path through the Village shone through. Aiden's broad shoulders and powerful arms were bare, and Tyler could imagine the light dusting of freckles on his forearms.

Beneath his own sheet, Tyler kicked off his boxers and spread his legs, bending his knees with feet flat on the mattress. As he stroked his cock steadily he caressed his nipples with the other hand, twisting and tweaking them until they were hard. Head turned on the pillow, he watched Aiden, knowing it was wrong but unable to stop.

He thought about what Aiden's mouth would taste like. He licked his lips, imagining the feel of Aiden's tongue against his. It was rare to get an opportunity to watch him uninterrupted—unseen. He drank in his bare flesh, kissing and touching it in his mind as he worked his own body, driving himself closer and closer to the edge.

Tyler sucked his fingers and pushed at his hole, biting his lip to stifle his cries as he imagined Aiden's cock inside him, driving him open and filling him. A moan escaped his lips as he squeezed in two fingers, and he held his breath, watching Aiden. But Aiden was still fast asleep.

It burned without any lube, but Tyler couldn't go to the bathroom for lotion because it would mean taking his eyes off Aiden. His dick was achingly hard and leaking, and he spread his knees wider, bracing as he thrust up into his hand. Thoughts tumbled scattershot through his mind as the pleasure built, rolling through his body.

*What if he wakes up? This is wrong. Or maybe he'll want it, too. Maybe he'll let me eat his cock and then climb on top of me and fuck me raw, fill me up and make me his—*

Tyler shuddered as his orgasm ripped free, splashing his chest and belly as he gasped, mouth open in silent bliss. He flopped his legs down and caught his breath, gaze still on Aiden. As the pleasure receded, guilt prickled at Tyler's skin. What was the matter with him? Aiden was never going to return his feelings—and why should he? Tyler was a kid who was probably just going to disappoint him and the team.

Now he was a pervert to boot.

He bet Greg Lewis never jerked off while watching Aiden sleep. With a shake of his head, Tyler retrieved his boxers and tiptoed to the bathroom to clean himself up. When he emerged a few minutes later, he froze in the doorway. He met Aiden's gaze and swallowed thickly. "Sorry. Did I wake you?"

Aiden rubbed his face and jerked his head toward the wall. "Nope. Who would have thought British equestrians were such party animals?"

His own heart was pounding so loudly in his ears that Tyler had to focus on the new *thumpa-thumpa* resonating from the room next door. He forced a smile and was glad he'd put his boxers back on. "I bet the Ukrainian weight lifters across the hall will have something to say about it, since they're competing tomorrow."

On cue, there was a pounding and raised voices from the hallway.

"Uh-oh," Aiden whispered. "I wouldn't want to get on the bad side of the weight lifters. Did you see that one guy's neck? It's bigger than my head."

They chuckled, and Tyler climbed back into bed as their end of the hall fell silent. "Let's hope that's the end of it. But I'm making a run to the drug store tomorrow for ear plugs. I'll pick you up a pair."

"Thanks. Normally I sleep like the dead. Hope I wasn't snoring or anything. After that last World Cup event, I wouldn't have been offended if you'd wanted your own room here."

"Don't worry about it. You had a cold." An unpleasant thought occurred. "Unless you wanted your own room?"

"No. It's... this is fine." Aiden yawned widely and stretched his limbs before curling onto his side away from Tyler. "'Night. Or, morning."

"'Night. Don't let the bedbugs bite." Tyler blushed as the little rhyme his mother used to say came out.

Aiden looked over his shoulder and grinned sleepily. "Please knock on wood immediately."

After rapping his knuckles against the table between their beds, Tyler settled back down. His earlier shame had dissipated, and this time he was asleep in minutes, thoughts of Aiden's smile floating through his mind.

# DIVE 4

*B*REATHE.

Tyler could feel the nervous tension in the crowd pulsing in the air—in his veins—like a living thing, as he and Aiden stood at the back of the platform for their running forward four-and-a-half somersault. They were still in the bronze medal spot, although the Mexicans were nipping at their heels. They couldn't afford to miss.

"Ready?"

"Yeah."

"One, two, three—up."

They rose to their toes, and Tyler ignored the throbbing.

"Go."

Their approach was a kind of skip into a powerful two-foot hurdle at the end of the platform that launched them up into the forward somersaults. Tyler clutched his knees to his chest as he rotated through the air and stretched out, pointing his battered toes before entry.

He went in at a slight angle, his heart sinking as he kicked to the surface. Yet the crowd's cheering seemed impossibly loud, so maybe it hadn't been that bad. Their coaches whistled, and Tyler pressed his lips together, ignoring the pain flaring all over his body. When the marks flashed up, he sighed in relief. Still third.

He dunked himself in the hot tub and sat back gingerly. Next to him, Aiden rested his hand on Tyler's shoulder, squeezing gently. For a moment, Tyler concentrated on the warmth of Aiden's palm and forgot about everything else. His fingers lingered, and Tyler leaned into the touch.

"Two more," Aiden whispered.

*Two days earlier*

"YES! THAT WAS your best yet!" Steve clapped on the pool deck. "You guys got this."

When they climbed out of the water, Aiden gave Tyler a perfunctory fist bump, and Tyler's excitement ebbed. They'd been diving better than ever, but Aiden didn't seem to share Steve's confidence.

"All right, hit the showers and go back to the Village. I'll meet you in the morning. Keep your eyes on the prize." Steve gave them both a hearty slap on the back.

It was the end of the night, and they were the last team left. Since the Olympic pool was occupied with events, they had practiced in a local pool. The shower room was empty as Tyler and Aiden padded inside.

Tyler turned on one of the showers and adjusted the temperature. "Damn, that was a great practice. I really think we can medal."

Aiden turned on his own shower nearby. "We'll see."

Jaw clenching, Tyler exhaled sharply. "Fine, forget it. We're gonna suck."

Aiden blinked. "What? What's wrong?"

Tyler roughly lathered shampoo into his hair. "Nothing."

"Tyler." Aiden watched him, brow furrowed, eyes kind. He waited.

After rinsing his hair, Tyler took a deep breath. "I know I'm not the partner you wanted to be here with. I'm not a vet like Greg. I've only *been* to one world championship, and he's *won* two. But I've been working my ass off for the past six months to make our team a success, and I'm sick of feeling like a disappointment."

Aiden stared, mouth open. "A *disappointment*?"

Tyler shrugged. "I know you don't think we can medal. If Greg was still competing—"

"Greg was a liar and a cheat," Aiden bit out. He

stepped closer, gaze steady. "I beat myself up constantly because I hadn't improved the way he did the last year. All he talked about was winning, and how I needed to keep up and get those extra inches of elevation. He offered me the new 'vitamins' he was using."

Tyler's hatred for Greg Lewis intensified. "Son of a bitch."

"Yeah. He would have taken me down with him if he had his way." Aiden ran his hand through his hair and blew out a long breath. "I thought he was my friend, and he was using *steroids*. I didn't want to believe it, but I knew deep down. That's why I didn't touch the pills he gave me. Jesus, Tyler. You have no idea how glad I am you're *not* Greg."

"I…" Tyler shook his head. "Why didn't you say anything?"

"I trusted Greg, and he betrayed me. I couldn't let that happen again. I thought if you and I just came to the pool and did our jobs without getting attached, it would be better that way."

"So… I'm not a disappointment?"

"No!" Aiden took a step closer, eyes imploring. "The farthest thing from it. I didn't want to pressure you. I think we can totally medal if we dive our best, but it's easy in practice. When you're standing up there with the whole world watching, you never know what can happen. One missed entry and it's over—the competition is too stiff. It's so easy to get rattled. But you're amazing. You've worked so hard and done so well. You're—" He broke off and stepped back.

"What?" Tyler snagged Aiden's wrist, and it was as if he'd touched a light socket as tingles flowed through his body.

Aiden's chest rose and fell. "I didn't want to get close. I tried to keep it just professional. It's not right. You're young, and I shouldn't... we shouldn't." He licked his lips. "Do you...?"

Body thrumming, Tyler hauled Aiden against him and they kissed, mouths opening, tongues meeting. They groaned and stumbled to the wall, Tyler's back against the wet tiles. The hot showers filled the room with steam as they rubbed against each other, kissing desperately.

Tyler's head spun, and he gripped Aiden's hips. They were already practically naked in their Speedos, and it only took a couple of tugs to free their hardening cocks. Aiden broke their kiss and wrapped his hand around their shafts, rubbing them together as he thrust his hips.

As his groan echoed off the slick tiles, Tyler pressed his lips together and hoped no one in the changing room had heard him. Aiden teased Tyler's nipples with his free hand and rested their foreheads together as he worked their cocks. Tyler's balls were tightening already. He didn't want this to end, and he grabbed Aiden's hand. "I'm gonna…"

But Aiden kept stroking and reached down with a wet finger to caress behind Tyler's balls and circle his hole. Tyler gasped, his cock throbbing.

"Let me see you come," Aiden whispered.

He didn't need to be asked twice. With a soft cry, Tyler came over Aiden's hand and spurted onto their stomachs, pleasure shuddering through him. Aiden milked him through several intense waves until Tyler could only whimper.

"You're so beautiful." Aiden pressed kisses to Tyler's flushed face. "Wanted this for so long."

In the steamy room, the haze of Tyler's orgasm seemed thick in the air. But he shook it off and spun them around, pressing Aiden back as Tyler sank to his knees. "Do you want this, too? I've thought about how your cock would taste every day."

Nodding jerkily, Aiden breathed heavily and tangled his fingers in Tyler's short hair. His bathing suit was tight around his thighs, and Tyler peeled it down so Aiden could step out of it and spread his legs. Their Speedos left little to the imagination, and of course Tyler had seen Aiden naked in the locker room.

But not like *this*.

Aiden's engorged cock was long and thick, with a gentle curve. Tyler kissed the tip, teasing at the slit with his tongue as Aiden groaned. Licking and sucking, Tyler worshipped Aiden's cock. He took it into his mouth, hollowing his cheeks as he sucked.

He didn't want this to be over yet, so he pulled off, grinning at Aiden's frustrated huff. Tyler caressed Aiden's smooth thighs and played with his heavy balls, rolling them together in his hands.

"Jesus, Ty." Aiden stroked Tyler's wet hair.

Tyler reached back to touch Aiden's hole, but it wasn't enough. He'd fantasized about this but had never done it with anyone, and before he could lose his nerve, he urged Aiden around to face the wall. As he spread Aiden's cheeks, he blew air over Aiden's sensitive flesh.

Moaning, Aiden open his legs wider and pushed his ass back toward Tyler's face. "Fuck. Yes. *Please.*"

With a deep breath, Tyler dove in, swirling his tongue around Aiden's hole. Tyler worked him open with his lips and tongue until he was inside that tight passage. Aiden's legs trembled and his harsh pants seemed loud in the empty shower room, bringing Tyler's dick back to life.

He wanted to stand and thrust into Aiden, fuck him and spill deep inside him, and then get down on his hands and knees and let Aiden do the same to him. But they didn't have condoms—and shit, someone was going to come looking for them sooner rather than later.

Reluctantly leaving Aiden's red, glistening ass, Tyler spun him back around and swallowed his cock. A few moments later, Aiden gripped Tyler's hair and shot into his mouth. Eyes closed with his head tipped back, mouth open, Aiden had never been so beautiful. Tyler swallowed as much as he could, milking Aiden until he was spent.

Aiden slid down the wall and collapsed in a graceless heap, with Tyler kneeling between his splayed legs. Reaching out, Aiden swiped his thumb across Tyler's swollen bottom lip, then tugged him close for a kiss. Their tongues slid together gently, and Tyler sighed.

When they broke apart again, Tyler pressed their foreheads together. "Keep thinking I'll wake up any second."

Aiden rubbed their noses together briefly, an easy smile—a *real* smile—brightening his face. "I thought… God, I'm an idiot. I thought it would ruin everything if you knew how much I wanted you. After Greg I was so determined to not get close again. Then you came along."

The question he hadn't wanted to ask escaped Tyler's lips. "You and Greg… Were you…?"

Aiden's unexpected laughter echoed off the tile. "Hell, no. Greg's as straight as they come. But I thought he was my friend. I trusted him. I didn't want to make the same mistake again. Then of course I fell for you. *Hard.*"

"You did, huh?" Tyler grinned and kissed him again. "Tell me more about that. No detail too small. Because I fell for you the day we made our first dive together."

"Oxford and Bourne?" A loud male voice rang out. "Pool's closing. Your transport's waiting."

Stifling their laughter, Tyler and Aiden scrambled to their feet, and Tyler called, "Coming!"

Of course this just made them laugh harder, and Aiden pulled him close for another kiss. "Twice, in fact," he murmured.

Tyler wanted so much to ignore the outside world and stay in the shower room with Aiden. He groaned. "I guess we'd better go."

"Yeah." Aiden turned off the showers. In the silence, he whispered, "I don't think it would go over so well if we got busted and kicked out of the Olympics for fucking in the facilities."

Tyler chuckled. "Can you imagine the headlines? The *Sun* would have a field day."

"Seriously. 'Dirty Diving Duo Ditched from Games.'"

They laughed and shared one last quick kiss before they got back to business.

# DIVE 5

HIS HEELS HANGING over the edge of the platform, Tyler raised his arms. The back two-and-a-half somersault, two-and-a-half twist in the pike position was one of his favorite dives to train. He took comfort in it now, even as his toes screamed.

"Up." Aiden paused as they raised their arms at their sides to shoulder height. "Ready?"

"Yeah."

"One, two, three—go."

Knees bending, arms pumping, Tyler shoved off, twisting and rolling through the air, keeping his legs locked and straight in a pike. It felt clean as he entered the water, and the crowd seemed to agree.

As he put his hands flat on the deck to push himself up out of the pool, his back protested, and he stumbled. But Aiden was there with a strong hand on his arm, steadying him.

"I'm fine." Tyler tried to smile, but it felt more like a grimace.

Aiden kept his hand where it was as they walked slowly to the hot tub. Tyler sank down under the water, willing his aching body to relax. The audience cheered, and he glanced at the marks and standings.

## 3. OXFORD Aiden / BOURNE Tyler

The Chinese were still first and couldn't be caught. But the Americans in second were only half a point ahead. Tyler took a deep breath, doing mental calculations to factor in the degree of difficulty of their next dive. At the thought of the remaining dive, Tyler's stomach churned.

"It doesn't matter."

Tyler blinked at Aiden. "Huh?"

"It doesn't matter where we end up." Aiden reached down and squeezed Tyler's hand quickly. "As long as we finish together. No disappointment."

One more dive. The only problem was that he didn't know if he could do it.

*One day earlier*

"*AGAIN.*" STEVE CALLED from the deck. "Tyler, your tuck is sloppy. Aiden, you're a beat too fast on the takeoff. What's up with you two today?"

As Steve and their coaching team muttered to each other, Tyler and Aiden shared a guilty glance and headed back up the stairs to the top of the platform. While they were still diving better than most teams in the world, Tyler knew their coaches were right. They had less than twenty-four hours until the competition, and they had to focus.

It was his fault—if he'd just bitten his tongue about how he was feeling, he and Aiden would never have talked, which of course had led to the sex.

They'd lasted all of thirty seconds, alone in their room at the Village, before they were tearing each other's clothes off, kissing and sucking each other until they were spent. They'd forced themselves to sleep in their own beds and get some rest, but even now as they climbed the tower, Tyler had to fight the urge to touch.

Part of him was giddy with joy. He couldn't believe it was real, that Aiden actually wanted him, too. But they had to keep their heads in the game. When they reached the top of the platform, Tyler spoke quietly. "Okay, from here on in until the competition's over, we're all business. Even when we're alone. We can't mess this up when we're this close."

Aiden nodded and held out his hand. "Deal."

Tyler slapped his palm lightly in their customary way. Okay, time to focus. This was the Olympics, and everything else could wait. On Aiden's command, they walked to the edge of the platform. Facing forward, toes at the end of the concrete, Tyler followed Aiden's cues and they exploded into the air in unison, somersaulting backwards—

*Smack!*

Toes burning, flames tore through his body, his lungs seizing. Where was he in the air—where was the water? Unfurling, he plummeted out of control—Jesus, *where was the water?*

Agony seared through his back as he hit the water and plunged beneath the surface. *Kick! Move! Air!* Stars filled his vision, black around the edges closing in…

Strong arms wrapped around him, and he tried to keep his eyes open as he was pulled upwards. Steve and the coaches were there in the water, and Tyler tried to focus on what they were saying, but he couldn't. *What happened?*

"Aiden, let go of him. We got this." Steve's voice was too loud.

The arms around him—Aiden's arms—tightened, and Tyler leaned against him and closed his eyes. Aiden was there. Everything would be okay. Then he was out of the water and there were more hands and voices, and the fog began to lift. Blinking, Tyler realized he was lying on the pool deck. His back and toes throbbed. A light filled his eyes.

As the medic examined him, a hand took hold of Tyler's. He knew it was Aiden's, and Tyler squeezed as hard as he could. "I'm fine," he said, although it sounded weak to his own ears. God, what had he done? He'd ruined everything after all without even having a chance to compete.

Aiden leaned over him, face pinched, eyes glistening. "You will be. It's okay. I'm right here."

As they put Tyler in a neck brace and onto a back board, then into a waiting ambulance, Aiden gripped his hand, never letting go once. Aiden had a brief argument with Steve about riding with Tyler, and Steve agreed to meet them at the hospital. The ambulance's siren was piercing, and Tyler tried to smile. "Think they can turn that down? I have a bit of a headache."

"Need those earplugs, huh?" Aiden's smile was shaky. He squeezed Tyler's hand and pressed a kiss to his forehead.

The hospital was a whirlwind of tests and doctors. Aiden finally had to let go of Tyler, and Tyler could hear him telling Steve outside the X-ray room that he didn't care that he was only wearing his Speedo.

When Tyler saw him again, Aiden was wearing his Olympic uniform of T-shirt and pants, and a pair of flip-flops. His hair had dried haphazardly and stuck up at odd angles.

He'd never looked so gorgeous.

Tyler found himself grinning as Aiden and Steve came into the exam area. "Looks like Steve finally won a battle today."

Steve shook his head, exasperated. "It took some

doing, let me tell you. How are you feeling, kid?"

*Like I fell ten meters onto concrete.* "I'm fine. Good to go. Right, doc?"

The doctor smiled as she pulled the curtain behind her. "You're very lucky, Tyler. No broken bones aside from the fifth toe on your right foot, which will heal on its own. Plenty of bruises though. Your back will be very sore for the next few days or longer. You grazed the tops of your toes against the concrete platform, so they'll be quite sore as well. I'd tell you to rest with your feet elevated, but somehow I doubt that's going to happen."

"I can still compete?" Tyler could hardly believe his luck.

The doctor tapped her pen on the clipboard. "It's up to you. You're going to be in pain, but your head and neck CT are clear. You're lucky that you don't have a concussion. Medically, you're able to compete if you choose. But there is still a risk you could injure yourself further.

"No, I'm good." Tyler wanted to laugh with joy, but his back twinged. "I'm competing."

"Ty, it's okay." Aiden stood with his hands jammed into his pockets, his brow furrowed as usual. "We'll see how you feel tomorrow."

The doctor signed his chart. "In the meantime, ice and take six hundred milligrams of ibuprofen three times daily. I'm sure your team knows what to do." She smiled. "Good luck, Tyler. We're all rooting for you."

"Thanks, Doc." Steve nodded to her. "Tyler, we'll reassess in the morning. I'll go call the van."

As soon as Steven was gone, Aiden was at Tyler's side, reaching for him. He brushed Tyler's hair back from his forehead. "I don't want you to hurt yourself. We don't need to compete."

"The hell we don't. I'm fine. I don't know what the hell happened. Everything was normal and then there was just pain and I lost my bearings. I'm sorry."

"Don't be sorry. It's my fault. We were both distracted."

"I'm fine, Aiden. We'll just keep to what we said earlier. All business until the competition is over. I can do this." His body ached in ways he hadn't known possible, but Tyler smiled. "I can do this," he repeated.

"Okay. All business." Aiden leaned down and kissed him gently, cupping Tyler's cheek. He pulled away and traced his fingertips over Tyler's lips. "Starting now."

# DIVE 6

"**W**ALK."

Tyler's breath came in short pants, his pulse racing too fast.

*You've done this dive a million times. Nothing's changed. It's another day at the pool.* Yet as Tyler took his position at the end of the platform, facing forward this time to launch himself into a reverse three-and-a-half somersault, panic flapped its wings. His breath hitched, and his mind filled with a jumble of images and emotions from training the day before, of falling out of control.

Beside him, Aiden hesitated as if sensing something was wrong. After a few beats, he asked, "Ready?"

His standard response died on his lips. Tyler's throat felt like sandpaper. A murmur traveled through the crowd, and Tyler forced his lungs to expand. Pain seared his ribs and he fought the urge to turn tail and run.

Under his breath, Aiden whispered. "I'm right here."

Tyler closed his eyes for a moment and inhaled before blowing the air out. A taut silence settled over the pool, the audience sensing something was amiss.

"Ready?"

Tyler swallowed hard. "Yeah."

"Up."

He raised his arms to shoulder height in unison with Aiden. Tyler wished he could close the gap between them and touch Aiden's fingers just for a moment.

"Ready?"

"Yeah." This was it. His nostrils flared. He could do this. He *would* do this.

"One, two, three—go."

Bending down into his knees, Tyler thrust himself up and off the platform as far as he could and into the backwards somersault. He hugged his knees to his chest, spinning tightly before entry. As he sliced into the water on the vertical, pride and relief swirled through him.

*I did it. We did it!*

The crowd was on its feet, cheering and shouting, the Canadian team screaming in joy. As he swam to the side of the pool, Tyler caught a glimpse of Nathalie and Audrey, standing on their seats and waving Maple Leafs. Then Aiden was there, his arms around Tyler, his breath warm in Tyler's ear as their legs tangled together below the surface.

"I love you."

They had to get out of the pool, and Tyler's head spun as he pushed himself up. On the deck, Steve and their coaches were there for a flurry of hugs and pats, and congratulations on a job well done.

The crowd hadn't stopped cheering, but suddenly erupted to a decibel level that shot through Tyler's body like a bolt of lightning. He grabbed Aiden's arm as they peered at the scoreboard.

*2. OXFORD Aiden / BOURNE Tyler*

"Silver!" Steve shouted, whooping. "*Silver!*"

Tyler was swept up into another round of hugs as the Mexicans waited atop the platform for the pandemonium to die down. They were out of medal contention after a miss on their fourth dive, so it was official.

"We won the silver medal." Tyler said it almost to himself, utterly disbelieving. The last dive had been almost perfect, with scores of 9.5 across the board for synchronicity.

Brown eyes sparkling and a grin lighting up his face, Aiden pulled Tyler into another hug. "Thank you."

They waved to their parents in the stands, and Tyler felt as though he had to be dreaming. He followed Aiden to the showers in a daze and rinsed off under the warm spray. He was an Olympic medalist. *They* were Olympic medalists. They grinned at each other and hugged again, not caring what anyone thought.

When he and Aiden climbed the podium, Tyler didn't feel an ounce of pain.

# EPILOGUE

★★ 🏊 ★★

STRETCHING GINGERLY, TYLER awakened. He was stiff and sore, but the memory of the day before dulled the ache. Judging by the light in the room, it was midmorning—the latest he'd slept in a long, long time. It felt strange not to have to get up and rush to the pool for practice. Of course, Aiden had to prepare for the singles competition the following week. But at least for this one day, they could relax.

Blinking, he focused on Aiden sitting on the other bed by the window. Aiden leaned back against the wall and gazed outside, wearing just an Adidas tank and his St. Sebastian medal. Stubble darkened his cheeks and his hair was rumpled. Tyler found himself smiling as he watched.

They'd spent the night in each other's arms in Tyler's bed, kissing and touching gently before giving in to their elated exhaustion. For a moment, squinting into the sunlight as he watched Aiden,

Tyler was afraid he'd see the old sadness again. His voice was gravelly from sleep. "You know I love you, too."

Aiden turned, his cheeks dimpling as a beautiful smile bloomed over his face. "I know. Just took me a little while to figure it out. How are you feeling?"

"Okay. Sore. But I'll live." Tyler stifled a wince as he climbed out of bed. He was naked, and Aiden's eyes darkened as his gaze raked over Tyler's body. Their medals sat on the table between the beds, and Tyler ran his fingertips over them before putting his back on around his neck. The silver was cool against his bare chest.

"That's a good look for you." Aiden licked his lips.

"Yeah?" Tyler ran his hand down his chest, past the medal and skimming over his belly and his morning hard-on. "You like?"

Aiden nodded. "C'mere."

Tyler knelt on the bed and reached out to stroke Aiden's thigh with a teasing smile. "Ready?"

Aiden chuckled. "Yeah."

"Up." Tyler tugged at Aiden's tank top, and Aiden raised his arms.

They were kissing before either could count to three.

## The End

**Read more sizzling sports romance from
Keira Andrews**

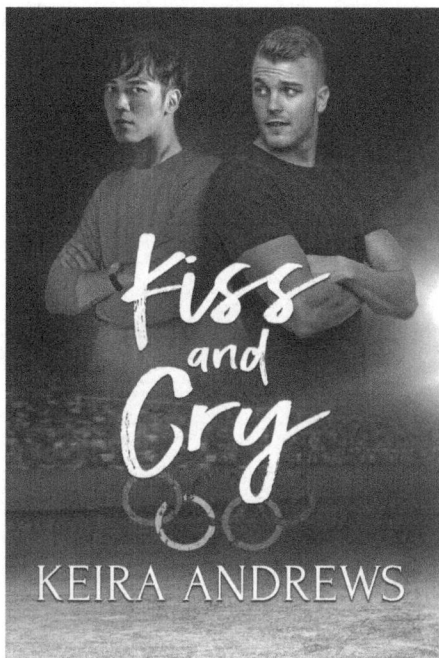

**Will figure skating enemies become lovers?**

**Henry**

Everything comes easily for Theo Sullivan, whether it's jumps or figure skating world titles. Everyone loves him—judges, fans, coaches.

I hate him.

Now he's invaded my training center, and I have to

see him every day as we prepare for the Olympics. I'm going to win gold if it's the last thing I do. I'm going to beat him.

But the strangest thing is happening. I'm peeking under his happy-go-lucky exterior and discovering there's more to Theo than I imagined.

This is a mistake. I can't trust him.

I can't be falling in love.

**Theo**
My mom's convinced training with Henry Sakaguchi will distract me heading into the Olympics. No way—Henry's epically boring and cold. He might as well be carved from ice.

But when I need help, he's there. He tries to keep me at arm's length, but it's no use. He's too kind. Too generous. He's caring and gorgeous and *hot*, and I've never wanted anyone like this.

I might want Henry more than a gold medal.

Am I falling in love?

*Kiss and Cry* by Keira Andrews is a steamy gay sports romance featuring opposites attracting, enemies to lovers, secretly soft-hearted boys, hurt/comfort, and of course a happy ending.

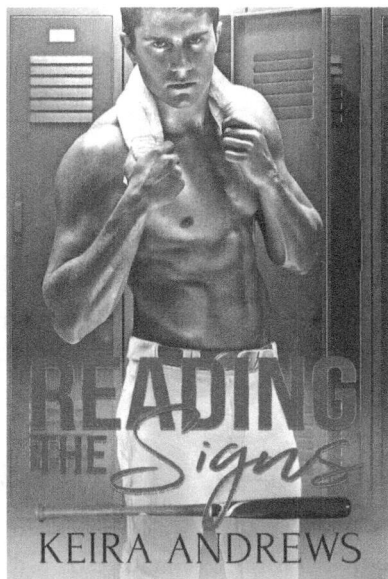

**This hot-headed rookie needs discipline—on and off the field.**

Pitcher Nico Agresta decided a long time ago he can never act on his desire for men despite a hopeless crush on his big brother's teammate Jake Fitzgerald. Nico is desperate to live up to his Italian-American family's baseball legacy, and if he can win Rookie of the Year in the big leagues like his dad and brother, maybe he can prove he's worthy.

At 34, veteran catcher Jake just wants to finish out his contract and retire. He lost his passion for the game—and life—after driving away the man he loved. He swore he'll never risk his heart again.

Then he's traded to a team that wants a vet behind the plate to tame their new star pitcher.

Jake is shocked to find the gangly kid he once knew has grown into a gorgeous young man. Tightly wound Nico's having trouble controlling his temper in his quest for perfection and needs a firm hand. Jake fights to teach him patience and restraint on the mound—but when the push and pull explodes off the field, can they control their hearts?

*Reading the Signs* by Keira Andrews is a gay sports romance featuring athletes repressing their feelings, first times and exploration, an age difference, and of course a happy ending.

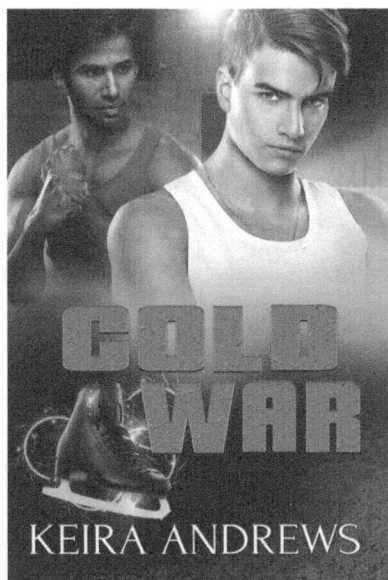

**Enemies on the ice. Forbidden lovers in the locker room.**

American figure skater Dev despises his Russian rival. Arrogant, aloof Mikhail is like a machine on the ice—barely ever making a mistake.

He's also sexy as hell, which makes him even more infuriating.

Dev and his pairs partner have been working their whole lives to become Olympic champions. He needs to keep his head in the game.

The very worst thing he could do is have explosive hate sex with Mikhail in the locker room after losing to him yet again before the Olympics.

But you know what would be even worse? Discovering that under Mikhail's icy exterior, he's *Misha*. Passionate and pent-up, he eagerly drops to his knees. His sweet smile makes Dev's heart sing, and his forbidden kisses are unbearably tempting.

Dev must resist.

But he's falling in love.

Only one of them can stand atop the podium. To win gold, will they lose their hearts?

*Cold War* by Keira Andrews is a gay sports romance featuring enemies to lovers, forbidden hookups blooming into a secret romance, opposites attracting, and of course a happy ending.

## About the Author

Keira aims for the perfect mix of character, plot, and heat in her M/M romances. She writes everything from swashbuckling pirates to heartwarming holiday escapism. Her fave tropes are enemies to lovers, age gaps, forced proximity, and passionate virgins. Although she loves delicious angst along the way, Keira guarantees happy endings!

**Discover more at:**
**www.keiraandrews.com**

Made in United States
Cleveland, OH
21 May 2025

17045438R00038